Otto

THE BOOK BEAR
in the Snow

KATIE CLEMINSON

JONATHAN CAPE
LONDON

Otto was a book bear. He lived in a book on a shelf in a library with his good friend Ernest.

Each night, when all was quiet, Otto and his friends would climb out of their books and explore the library.

One night Otto found everyone busily
making colourful decorations.
  "What's happening?" he asked.
  "It's our special winter party soon," Ernest
told him. "I can't wait for you to see it."

But the *very* next morning
Otto and Ernest's book was

taken off the shelf,   stamped,

packed   and carried across town.

They had been borrowed!

Otto and Ernest were read every night
and they felt very happy.

But as time went by, Otto and Ernest became
a bit worried that they wouldn't be back
in time for the winter party.

What was worse, one day they found a pile of suitcases in the hall. The family were going away on holiday . . .

Soon Otto and Ernest were alone!

Ernest was terribly upset — the library was all the way across the city, which was a very long way for two book bears to carry their book.

Otto knew there had to be a way to get back.

He started to think of a plan.

Suddenly he had a brilliant idea. "Don't worry, Ernest — we can POST ourselves home!"

Otto packed his trusty bag, Ernest found envelopes and stamps,

and together they set off.

They made their way out of the house . . .
across gardens . . . along pathways . . .
until eventually they found a postbox.

As they climbed in,
                    snowflakes started to fall.

Before long the postman arrived

and bundled them
into a sack,

and they were
sorted, stamped,

bagged and
packed,

and back on the
road again.

But moments later —

CRASH!

The bag they were in had fallen off
the bicycle and into the snowy road.

Ernest grabbed
Otto just in time.

"Well, that was a close call," said Otto.
"Thank you, Ernest."
"But what will we do now?" asked Ernest.

"Don't worry — we'll just have to walk,"
replied Otto, picking up their book
and bravely setting off into the snow.

Now it was getting dark.
The snow was heavier and deeper.

Otto and Ernest walked and walked,
and it soon became clear that . . .

. . . they were lost.

"We're never going to get home!"
said Ernest. "Never mind being
in time for the party."

"Don't give up, Ernest!
I'm sure something will
come along soon," said Otto.
In the distance a figure
appeared through
the snow. A dog!

"Please don't eat us!" said
Ernest to the large dog.
"We're lost and can't
get home to the
library," said Otto.
"Can you help?"

The dog lay down on the snow
beside them and told them to
climb on his back —
he would see what he could do.

They travelled down busy bright streets

and under high bridges, down long alleyways,

racing through the dark night . . .

Together they ran and ran,

until they were *finally* back at the library steps.

But had they missed the party?

Not at all!
Otto's first winter party
was in full swing . . . and what
a party it was!

As they climbed up to their bookshelf, Ernest said, "I'm so happy to be home, Otto. I love being read, but I think I want to stay here for a little while."

Otto sleepily agreed, but he also couldn't help thinking how much he had loved adventures —

seeing the falling snow, and riding through the city at night. In fact . . .

big adventure soon!

For Isla Rose

JONATHAN CAPE

UK | USA | Canada | Ireland | Australia
India | New Zealand | South Africa
Jonathan Cape is part of the Penguin Random House group of companies
whose addresses can be found at global.penguinrandomhouse.com.
www.penguin.co.uk   www.puffin.co.uk   www.ladybird.co.uk

Penguin
Random House
UK

First published 2016
001
Copyright © Katie Cleminson, 2016
The moral right of the author has been asserted

Printed in China
A CIP catalogue record for this book is available from the British Library

ISBN: 978–1–780–08011–6

All correspondence to:
Jonathan Cape, Penguin Random House Children's, 80 Strand, London WC2R 0RL